“Tansy Joy & Too Many Tangles

By Niccole Perrine

ISBN: 9781086825534

Niccole Perrine, Author
alabasterjarlr@gmail.com

Dedicated to my amazingly patient husband, Luke, and our five little joys, LB, RT, IE, ED, & IM. You are the best and sweetest gifts God has blessed me with and I praise Him for you daily. I love you "*all done.*"

Table of Contents

CHAPTER ONE

Tansy Joy was hiding under her bed. Her nose wrinkled up as she lay there, looking just beyond the edge of her soft pink blanket. She knew eventually, she would have to come out from underneath her bed. But she figured, maybe, if she stayed put long enough, that by the time she finally surfaced, it would be too late.

See, Tansy had a problem. She had too many curls. She sighed loudly as she smelled the savory bacon and heard Mom in the kitchen, probably making biscuits and eggs to go with the bacon. She hoped that Mom would remember that she liked her eggs so that she could pop the yolk. Tansy hated it when she couldn't pop the yolk. That was half the fun of eating eggs for breakfast. So much better than the days Mom made oatmeal. She sighed uncomfortably, as Sulky padded into the room.

"Shoo!" Tansy whispered, looking into Sulky's eyes. The cat walked up to her, sniffed the air, then sat and started grooming himself. He was completely unconcerned about his owner's plight. His short, gray fur had a healthy shine and he took great pains to make sure every effort was made to keep himself handsome.

Tansy thought about this a while. Then, shifting a bit, she thought about her more-immediate problem. Everyone that Tansy knew, (even her little sisters) had straight, smooth or gentle, wavy hair. Well okay, if Tansy had to be honest...and she tried her best to be honest...*Mom* had curly hair. But *Moms* didn't count. Not when you had to sit and get your hair combed and styled and pulled. No, Mom hair was *completely* different and didn't count one bit, as for as Tansy was concerned.

It was the first day of July. Tansy, her big brother Zeb, and the twins, Flora and Fauna were all supposed to start their *Summer Bucket List today. (*If you've never heard of a *Bucket List*, then I'll tell you about it. A *Bucket List* is a list of activities that you want to do before you "kick the bucket"; that means to die, usually. Which was kind of silly, because everyone in the Joy family was in good health.) Nevertheless, Mr. and Mrs. Joy had a tradition that every summer, the Joys would have a family meeting and create their *Summer Bucket List.* This year they were getting a late start on their annual tradition due to June having been unusually rainy for the small desert town of Vespa, Idaho.

In fact, it had been so rainy that all the trees had been late in bearing fruit this year. The big apricot tree in the Joys' back yard only had tiny little olive-shaped fruits on it still, and they were still green. Usually by July the fruit was juicy and falling off of the tree, making a big sticky mess in the yard. Mr. Joy particularly disliked the mess the fruit trees made. The Joy children loved to play outside in their imaginary forts and eat the fresh fruits as they ripened. There were actually a good many trees in the backyard; plum, peach, apricot, even a large grapevine grew along their fence. It was a good yard and the Joy children had spent countless hours there.

This year, with the unusually wet weather the Joy children felt that they had missed out on most of their summer activities. When the family had sat down for their annual family meeting, (just a few weeks earlier) they had made it a point to fill the list with things that would take place outside in the sunshine.

Here is what the Joy family list had on it so far:

Saddle Club

Farmer's Market

Water Park

Sunday School Picnic (Bring Lemonade!)

Go See 'Space Movie' in the park (Bring money for popcorn and snow cones!)

Since the weather was supposed to be dry and warm in July, Mr. Joy had decreed that July first would be the first day of summer for the family. (That was another nice thing that the Joy children loved, they didn't have to go to regular school, like most children.) They got to do school when the weather was bad and then play outside when the weather was nice. Mom and Dad called it a *year-round schedule* and they did it because it made the most sense. Since the Joy kids had always been schooled at home, they thought it was a marvellous idea. It was a good life indeed.

Tansy Joy heard her Dad coming down the hallway. It was a Friday, so she knew he was getting himself ready to go to work. They would all have breakfast together, do their chores, and finally, start the day's activities.

Mr. Joy worked in a city nearby. He was a safety inspector for the local train yard, and often had to work from late in the afternoon until well after the Joy children went to bed. Because he worked long and late hours, he made sure that mornings were extra special and that his days off were planned to include everyone. Tansy thought her Dad was probably the best dad ever.

"Tansy-Bear!" Dad called.

Tansy heard her Dad's voice and then saw his feet standing in front of her face. His socks were mis-matched, and his toes wiggled in front of Tansy's face. Sulky meowed in complaint and went out.

"I'm down here." Tansy said, her voice somewhat muffled from the bed above her.

Dad crawled down on his stomach to peer under the bed.

"Tansy! What are you doing? Don't you know it's nearly breakfast time?"

Tansy crawled out from under the bed, stretching her arms and legs. Dad was smiling at her. She took a big breath and said, rushing to get it out fast:

"*Didntwannadomyhairtoday.*"

Dad nodded. They had talked about this before; many times. His eyes were compassionate as he watched his daughter's tight chocolate curls bounce with each toss of her head.

"I know how you feel, pumpkin'. But it's gotta get done. Tell you what, why don't we go get breakfast first before we tackle your tangles? Come along, now."

Tansy followed along. She sat at breakfast and after giving thanks the family dug in. Zeb was loading up biscuits on his plate, two pieces of bacon having already been shoved in his mouth. He grinned, showing his food-filled teeth. Tansy scowled at him.

Flora and Fauna were chatting away at the other end of the table. They were discussing the day's plans. Today they were supposed to go to Saddle Club. It was their first day and they were very excited to join in with the other kids at *Dusty Ranch*. The Joy kids were friends with the owner's kids, Jeremy, Jane, and Elsie. It was going to be a good day.

"Apple butter?" Tansy's Mom asked, offering the

jar of sweet sauce to her oldest daughter.

"Sure, I guess." Tansy said. She sighed. Her stomach grumbled.

"Eat up," Mom said. "We need to get things done if we want to do Saddle Club."

CHAPTER TWO

Tansy looked with distaste at her set of combs and sighed. Breakfast had been cleared and the dishwasher was humming as the dishes were cleaned. Her Mom had told her to go and get ready for the day. This usually meant finding her shoes, something to wear, brushing her teeth, and washing her face. Those weren't so bad. It was brushing her hair that Tansy hated out of all of these.

Her curls were thick, like wool, or yarn. Dad often joked that they had a mind of their own. He loved Tansy's curls and often would tell Tansy to be thankful that she had such nice hair.

It wasn't so much that Tansy minded her curls. They came in handy when she wanted to look fancy, like at last year's Christmas pageant. No, they were very pretty. She was convinced there were just too many of them. She picked up a comb and started the work she knew that eventually Mom would have to finish.

"Don't forget to put some *goop* in." said Mom, as she checked her purse, making sure everything the family needed for the day was packed properly.

Tansy got the bottle of hair goop and put a small amount on her hands. It smelled nice. She rubbed her hands together and slowly added the goop to the bottom of her hair, working her way up to the top. The hair *goop* wasn't actually called that. It was a special hair oil that Mom had bought at the salon. The goop was supposed to help keep Tansy's hair from being too frizzy. Tansy's Mom was always trying to find ways to make Tansy love her hair and take better care of it.

"You know, when I was your age, I had the same trouble." Mom would start. "But my parents didn't know what to do with my curls and so it was a constant battle. I was almost twenty-four years old when I learned to love my curls."

"What happened when you were twenty four?" Tansy would ask.

She had heard her Mom tell the story many times, but it was a comfort to hear it just once more.

"That's when I had a precious little one come into my life." Mom would then smile softly. "And she had as many curls as I did!"

This was usually followed by a big bear hug. Tansy secretly thought her mom was a pretty amazing mom. But it would never do to tell her that. That would just be *awkward*. Instead, Tansy just hugged her mom back. She was happy to know that she was loved.

"Okay, Missy." Mom said. "Let's tackle the back. Why don't we try wearing it up today?"

Tansy grimaced. She *hated* wearing her hair up. It wasn't so much because of how it *looked*, but how it *felt*. Tansy's hair was not too long, just past her shoulders. But in the summer heat, having her hair up made the most sense. It just hurt when Mom put the elastics in. In fact, putting it up hurt, wearing it up hurt, and taking it out hurt. Not only did it hurt, but the elastics ripped her hair out. Sometimes, Tansy worried that the elastics would pull *all* of her hair completely out one day. She didn't want to be bald.

Mom started combing Tansy's tangles out with a special comb called a "wide-toothed-comb". She had told Tansy how hairbrushes really weren't good for her tight curls.

"They ruin the curl structure." she said. "Curly hair

is incredibly delicate. Almost as fine as a cobweb- even though all of it together feels and looks super thick."

Mom had read several books about curly hair since Tansy was born. She had learned different ways to style Tansy's curls and to make her own longer curls healthier and prettier. Reading to learn new things was probably what Mom loved best. Tansy privately thought that if Mom did less reading, they could do more important things, like go horseback riding, but as Dad often pointed out, "*Mom is Mom. You can't change her, you can only change you. Besides,"* he would ask." *Would you really want her to be anything but herself?"*

Tansy held on to her stuffed bear, Benny, as her Mom worked through her twisted tangles. Actually, the hair on top, called the *canopy,* wasn't too bad. But as Mom worked towards the back and the bottom, Tansy clutched her bear tighter and tighter. Her shoulders were tense and her head ducked down as Mom got closer and closer to what Mom said was not always, but in some cultures was called *the kitchen.*

The *kitchen* as you may or may not know, is the very back bottom of someone's hair, right at the nape of the neck. It's a term used in some American cultures to define the section of hair where the worst of tangles can be found, and is called this because it's where all the hard work gets done. Before Mom got to this most difficult section of Tansy's hair, she stopped.

"Let's take a break before we finish." Mom stood up and went to get a cup of coffee, adding cream and sugar and taking a slow sip. She waited a few moments, listening to Tansy's siblings laughing and playing in the yard.

Tansy's face was pink from holding her breath. She hugged her bear. She knew that as soon as the tangles were out the worst would be over with. She relaxed a little more as Mom finished her coffee.

"Alright," Mom said. "Let's get it done."

Tansy let her mom finish the job, wincing and complaining as quietly as she could manage. She didn't want to make her little sisters worry by yelling. She needed to be an example. Besides, she was pretty sure that most nine-year-olds didn't cry over hair.

Mom finished up by putting Tansy's hair in a tight bun right on top of her head. She used a black elastic and several bobby pins to secure it. The hairstyle was very tight, but it was also off of Tansy's neck, which was a good thing since they were going to be at Dusty Ranch all day and the sun was already beating down. The thermometer read ninety-degrees Fahrenheit. It was going to be what Granddad would have called a *scorcher.*

Tansy shook her head, experimentally. Sometimes, Tansy's bun wouldn't stay put and the bobby pins Mom used to hold the bun together would fall out, scattering everywhere. The hair stayed put. She gave her mom a quick hug and then ran out to join her sisters and brother. The sun was shining, and the day was getting on.

CHAPTER THREE

The Joy children arrived at Dusty Ranch that afternoon, excited and full of laughter. Both families of children were bouncing with energy as they greeted one another. As they waited for Saddle Club to begin, Tansy chattered good-naturally with Jeremy, Jane, and Elsie.

"Hey Jane!" Tansy said, grinning. "What book are you reading this week?"

"Elves, Dragons, and Mermaids- a Safari Guide." Jane said. "It's really great."

"Flora, can you help me with my helmet?" Tansy asked. "I can't seem to get it over this bun."

After some effort, the girls decided to take Tansy's hair down and braid it No matter how hard they tried, the tight bun just wouldn't fit under the helmet.

Dusty Ranch had several horses of different breeds and backgrounds, but *Saddle Club* was a special club for kids who wanted to learn about the care of the horses, their *tack*, and their environment. Each class was supposed to start with a lesson on horse care, then the students would practice grooming the horses, and at the very last, the students would each get to ride for a while on the horse of their choice.

Mr. and Mrs. Franzoso were very excited to be offering the new club for their students to enjoy. It was especially nice because it gave the kids a chance to connect and learn something together, outside of the regular lessons that the Franzoso family offered.

Today's lesson had to do with keeping the horses hooves clean of rocks and thorns. Mrs. Franzoso used a special tool to clean out the hoof, pointing out the soft *frog* that was inside the hoof. If the *frog* got anything stuck inside of it the offending item could make a horse go lame.

"No hoof, no horse." Mrs. Franzoso pointed out.

The Joy kids each had a turn helping groom the horses. Then they each lined up to take their turn on their favourite mount. When they were finished, Mrs. Franzoso told them about the plans for the following week.

"Next week, we're going to learn how to take care of our horses' manes, so make sure you think about what kinds of styles you want to try out. The person who has the best styled horse will win a special prize!"

Everyone thanked the teacher and then headed to the cool shade of the fire pit area for lemonade and cookies.

"What kinds of hairstyles do horses wear, anyway?" Asked Flora.

"Oh all kinds of braids and stuff," said Jane looking up from her book. Jane was thirteen and knew about everything. "The horse hair is really coarse but it can be done three different ways. It's actually a lot like human hair. It can be braided, twisted, or tied. Some people even combine all three. It's like artwork. You'll have to go to one of the horse shows or rodeos. There are some amazing styles people create, and shows are the best way to see what styles get the most attention." She bit into a Cowboy cookie and went back to her novel.

"Horse hair is like human hair?" Tansy giggled, imagining a great big horse, like her personal favourite, Tiny. Tiny was not a small horse, rather he was the largest horse at Dusty Ranch. Tansy loved the gentle *Percheron* gelding. She imagined herself washing and shampooing Tiny's dapple-gray coat and trying to comb out the tangles in his long white mane and tail. She looked over at the pasture where he was currently rolling in the tall green grass and sand. Great big dust clouds went up as he rolled. Tiny loved a good roll in the grass.

Jeremy cleared his throat and took a gulp of the ice-cold lemonade, before speaking. “Horses actually have three types of hair on their body that all feel different: mane, tail, and fur. Their mane hair feels a lot like human hair, soft, smooth and it can be shorter or longer. Maybe a little bit less silky because they don’t tend to use conditioner.” He grinned. “Their tail hair is also somewhat like human hair, just thicker. And I don’t mean in *volume,* like in the amount of hair. I mean the actual hair strands are larger, coarser, and thicker. So imagine somewhat breakable human hair. It’s not exact, but close enough.”

“How do you comb it?” asked Tansy. “Does it hurt?”

“First you have to look for junk that gets caught in the mane. Things that can really hurt the horse when you comb it out. Things like leaves, sap, sticks, even burrs or goat-heads can get caught in there. The horses can’t just pull things out themselves. They have no hands! Usually Mom is the one who does the brushing part. She used to buy a brush from the Tack Store, but now she just buys a regular boar-bristle brush to save on expenses. The vet says it's just as good and costs less. Even though it might look a little funny sometimes."

Tansy thought about this as she wiped her hands on her dusty jeans. It seemed that horses had hair problems just as much as she did.

CHAPTER FOUR

The next day was Saturday. Tansy woke up to the sound of her sisters arguing over which Saturday morning cartoons to watch. She rolled over and went to see what the fuss was about.

"I want to watch *Super Wild Sparkle Horse*." Explained Fauna. "Flora wants to watch *Mega Mario Racer.*

Flora's face was in a big pout. She really loved *Mega Mario Racer*. Tansy didn't really like it all that much, but it wasn't a good plan to start the morning off with an argument. Besides, today Mom and Dad were supposed to take the kids to the Farmer's Market and she didn't want to get into trouble and miss something special from the family *Bucket List* because of a dumb television program.

"Why don't we just set a timer and when it goes off, we can change the show?" asked Tansy. "It's not like we can't watch it any time we like."

The Joy family only had one television, and they didn't watch commercial TV. They instead paid for a subscription to watch movies and films that could be watched over and over again. Actually, that was probably why nobody except Flora wanted to watch *Mega Mario Racer*- it only had one season and the children had seen every episode already. Twice. Saturday mornings were the only mornings when the Joy children had permission to eat cereal in front of the TV and watch cartoons. They even got to watch cartoons *before* getting dressed.

The twins' argument was settled immediately, and they all started to watch *Mega Mario Racer.* It was the first episode and they got all the way through that and halfway through a new episode of Super *Wild Sparkle Horse* when Zeb walked into the living room. Zeb yawned and immediately started looking for his favourite cereal *Honey Bundles of Wheat.* He looked around for signs of Mom and Dad, making sure the coast was clear. Then instead of getting a bowl, Zeb simply put a fistful of cereal in his mouth, then took the milk jug and poured a little bit of that in as well. He crunched the cereal with a smile, milk dripping down the corners of his mouth.

"What's up Kids?" He asked. "Not watching *Super Wild Sparkle Horse* again, are you?" He rolled his eyes.

"Why do we always have to watch stuff for *babies?"* Even though he was only eleven, sometimes Zeb liked to pretend that he was much older and better than his sisters. Tansy looked over at her brother. She knew that sometimes he liked the program and sometimes he only *pretended* not to.

"*Shhh! Zeb*, it's a new episode!" Tansy whispered to him, not wanting to miss anything in the story. Zeb stopped complaining and for the rest of the program, all you could hear was the crunching of the cereal, the sound of the TV, and the occasional belch from Zeb. Eventually, Mom and Dad were up, and getting everyone ready to head to the Farmer's Market. The TV was turned off and the breakfast dishes were clear. Everyone was ready again except Tansy.

"It's not *fair."* She pouted. "Nobody else in this family understands me. I'm not like Flora and Fauna and Zeb doesn't even *have* hair.

Zeb's hair was a buzz cut. He hated having his blonde hair look like a haystack, so he had asked Dad to keep it short for him this summer.

"Hey," Zeb said. "Take it easy, Tans. If you were

my kid, I'd be happy to shave your head!"

Tansy scowled. "I don't want it shaved. I want it straight... or maybe just straighter. It won't tangle as much and I can make pretty styles like my friends do at *Saddle Club*." In particular, Tansy was thinking of Jane's slippery-smooth, nut-brown hair. It was the kind of hair that looked easy and it never seemed to get frizzy or tangled. Jane's hair was almost never up and she just wore it in long braids or down, like an almond waterfall. Tansy's hair just bunched up and frizzed up making her feel like she had a giant fur ball on her head most of the time.

As Tansy went through her morning hair-brushing routine, Mrs. Joy was thoughtful. Being nine was a challenge, she thought. Maybe it's time we did something about this.

"Besides the tangles, Tansy-Bear." She asked. "What is it you don't like about your hair?"

Tansy thought about this. She wasn't even sure if she knew what bothered her the most but did her best to share what was on her mind. "Well," she started. "It's not that I don't *like* my hair. I mean, it's pretty sometimes.

But… I hate it when it hurts me. I don't like having it so tight all the time. And when I'm riding Tiny, it doesn't fit in my helmet very well."

Mrs. Joy listened to this carefully and she quickly put Tansy's hair into two braids.

"Anything else?"

"Yeah, I mean, I want to have it *look* cool. It just seems like it has to be down or in this tight knot all the time. I don't like when it's shorter because then it's just too… boyish. I don't want to feel like I look like a boy. I want to look like what I am. A girl."

"A beautiful girl, beautifully created to be *you!*" Dad said as he came to give Tansy a hug.

"Thanks, Dad." Tansy said. "I just wish it was easier. I don't know if I'll ever get rid of all these tangles, but maybe if my head didn't hurt so much when I had it up, it wouldn't tangle so badly." She looked a little nervous as she added, "I don't want to go bald either. Those elastics rip my hair out!"

Mom and Dad chuckled.

"Well, I know it tears up your hair. " Mom said. "However, I don't think you'll be going bald anytime soon."

Dad looked at his daughter, eyes sparkling.

"Don't you want hair like dear old Dad?" He teased. Dad had once had thick black hair, the exact same color as Tansy's. As he had gotten older it had thinned out, leaving it not quite bald in some places but close enough that some might use the term.

"Dad…" Tansy groaned.

Mom smiled. "You know what? I heard one of the other parents at *Saddle Club* talking about a neat place at the Farmer's Market that I think we'll want to check out. Why don't we see if we can find it? They are supposed to have all kinds of pretty hair accessories and one gal was saying that they're supposed to work for every hair style."

Tansy thought about it and shrugged. "It sounds too good to be true."

Mom hugged her. "We'll never know until we ask."

CHAPTER FIVE

The *Vespa Farmer's Market* was the biggest in the whole county. Even though the town of Vespa was quite small, the location was ideal for all the surrounding farm communities. The Market was only open Saturdays each week and thousands of people would come from the cities and towns and even from across the Idaho State Line to walk, shop, and eat.

There were so many things to see, smell, and touch. When the Joy Family arrived to the Market, it was about mid-morning. The morning was bright and sunny with a hint of a breeze. It seemed like everyone in the whole valley had come out.

There were vendors selling all kinds of delicacies: doughnuts, sweet corn, roasted peanuts, home-canned sauces if you could think of it, there's a good chance you would find it. Each of the Joy kids got one of their favourite Farmer's Market snacks, a pork tamale from Pepe's. They enjoyed their spicy treats as they walked admiring all the various booths.

There were all kinds of people to see at the Market

as well. As the Joys left the avenue that had the food vendors, they entered the street that had the local produce. There were so many different people there selling the ripe vegetables and fruits. There was a sign that caught Mr. Joy's eye, so he quietly slipped some cash into Zeb's hand with a wink and Mrs. Joy was soon pleased and astonished to see Zeb come back with a whole crate of her favourite Ginger Gold apples.

Mr. Joy and Zeb went off to put the apples back into the van, while the girls looked around, taking in the sights. On the following avenue, there were booth vendors set up. People were selling homemade soaps and lotions, scarves and hats, knitted woollen scarves, there was even a booth that had hammered silver spoons made into pieces of jewellery and art.

Tansy loved the market. She thought it was one of the most interesting places ever. People were happy and smiling, walking their dogs of all shapes and sizes. There were musicians, both young and old, good and bad in the street, busking for coins. On one corner, a string quartet started playing the theme from a popular space movie.

As the girls turned another corner they spied a

bright purple tent. It was filled with ladies young and old, and small children, each straining to hear and see what was going on. In the centre of this crowd was a petite woman, with blonde hair and a big smile. She had the brightest purple dress Tansy had ever seen.

"Hello Ladies!" Purple Lady called out through her booth speakers. "I would love to help each and every one of you! Let me show you how these amazing clips work. And yes, they work for *all* hair styles, cuts, and textures! Better yet? They don't tear your hair out or cause those terrible tension headaches you get from traditional elastics. I'll need some volunteers to come up for the demonstration."

Mrs. Joy nudged Tansy. She whispered, "Tansy? Do you want to try them?"

Tansy looked up at the pretty blonde woman's hair. It wasn't anything like Tansy's hair. It was held with a beautiful metal clip in a half-up, half down style. Purple Lady's hair was baby-fine with that straight, smoothness that looked like delicate spider silk. In Tansy's experience, anything that was good in silky-straight hair wasn't likely to work with her thick, black curls.

Purple Lady spoke out again.

"Don't be shy, ladies! Let's see if we can get a variety of styles up here." She patted one of the three raised stools in front of the booth. "Here's what I'll do! All my volunteers will receive a *free* bobby pin for helping me out up here." She held up a beautiful silver bobby pin with a horse-shaped decoration on the end. The horse was raised on its hindquarters and seemed to dance on the pin as it caught the light. Tansy remembered what the Franzoso kids had said. *Horses hair is a lot like human's hair...* She thought about the special prize that would be to the best winner at Saddle Club that was being given away. She raised her hand.

"Come on up here!" Smiled Purple Lady looking right at Tansy. "Wowza! I wish I had hair like yours! It's so curly!"

"Thanks." Tansy said. She handed her gear to her mom and patiently waited while the lady gathered two other volunteers from the crowd. One girl was only a baby. Maybe a kindergartner. She had hair as white as corn silk, and you could almost see through it. It was as short as her chin and very, very soft looking. The other lady who sat with them was an older lady. The older lady had bright red hair all the way down to her ankles and it was wavy. She looked like she was really hot and wishing for the cooler weather from the month before. She smiled and Tansy thought, *Rapunzel, She looks just like Rapunzel from my bedtime story!*

"*This*," Purple Lady said, "Is a *Flexi-clip.* It's made from super-flexible piano wire on one side, and super-strong metal on the slotted pin side. The metal is made from the same material from which nuts and bolts are made." She held up a huge clip, it was shaped in a figure eight, and had beautiful turquoise beads accenting the clip. She demonstrated how strong it was by bending it nearly in half. After asking Rapunzel if she could touch her hair, she then took Rapunzel's hair and twisted it up into an elegant twist. Then she placed the pin of the clip underneath the twist, against the scalp, and bent the flexible, piano-wire part over Rapunzel's twisted hair. It was impressive. All that hair held with just one clip!

Rapunzel sat there with a look that was relief mixed with disbelief. She carefully reached up her hands to touch her hair.

“Why don’t you give it a shake?” Grinned Purple Lady.

“Are you sure?” Asked Rapunzel. Her eyes were as big as saucers.

“Go for it!” Purple Lady winked at Tansy.

Rapunzel shook her head.

“Shake it like ya mean it!” Said Purple Lady.

Rapunzel shook her head like she meant it. Then she shook it some more. She was laughing.

“I’ve never seen anything like it. Is this some kind of trick?”

Purple Lady got serious. “Not a trick. The clip clamps the hair to itself, so it stays in place and then it also will displace the weight more evenly across the head, meaning that you won’t have all that weight in one place, causing those headaches you probably hate.”

Rapunzel was amazed. “How much is it? Never mind. I want the one on my head and anything else you have to sell that will fit me.”

Purple Lady sent Rapunzel over to Purple Man to buy her hair clip. She smiled the whole time.

Next it was Tansy’s turn. She had watched

Rapunzel get her hair done and was getting nervous and excited. She worried a little that maybe it wouldn't work for her curly hair and that Purple Lady would be disappointed.

Purple Lady held up a fancy white and gold clip with a flower in the middle. "Now, folks, what you just saw me use on our first participant's hair was the Mega size hair clip. It's also called a double-ex-el. You might be wondering, how is something that fits someone with that much hair going to fit this beautiful young lady?"

The clip in her hand was much smaller than the turquoise clip that she had used before."This is the large and you can see it's size by looking on the grooved pin part, here.

She leaned toward Tansy. "May I style your hair?" Tansy nodded and waited to have her hair styled. She hoped she wouldn't cry in public.

CHAPTER SIX

Tansy Joy was smiling so big, her cheeks were starting to get sore. Not only was she feeling beautiful, but she had a sparkle in her eye and a spring in her step that even her Sunday School teacher noticed.

"My goodness Tansy Joy! You seem in such a good mood today! Mrs. Johnston smiled.

Tansy beamed back. She wanted to tell *everyone* the secret of her hair pretty, but Mom and Dad had asked the girls to not brag about their pretty new things in church. The Joy parents were very firm- showing off in church just wasn't what you did, church wasn't for showing off. They could enjoy their new pretties and be excited, but they weren't to brag.

The truth was, Tansy couldn't believe how happy she was. Not only had the beautiful hair pretties worked in her own hair, they had worked for all the Joy ladies. Mrs. Joy had been so impressed with the Purple Lady's booth, that she had immediately bought Tansy, Flora, and Fauna each a clip of their choice, as well as had a hushed conversation with Purple Lady.

"I'll be in touch." She had said, with a mysterious grin that only Dad seemed to understand.

The Joys had finished their day at the Farmer's Market and went home. Tansy felt like all her hair problems would be so much better now that her hair was so comfortable in its beautifully styled bun on her head. Purple Lady (whose real name was Miss Shoshanna, but she would forever be *Purple Lady* in Tansy's mind) had told Tansy she was going to do something called a forty-second French twist. And before Tansy could yell "Cat!" her hair was in a beautiful bun with a few curls showing out the sides.

Now it was Sunday afternoon, she had her hair up, and it was time to figure out her next problem. She wanted very badly to win that "special prize" that Mrs. Franzoso had offered. Somehow, she knew that she would not be able to do a French twist in her horses' mane. So instead, with permission from Mom and Dad, she went to the family computer and started her research. Using the *browser,* which is a fancy tool for searching for stuff, she typed in some words that lead her to the information she was searching for.

Every time Tansy typed in a word; she would click on a website that said it had information about the word Tansy typed in. She had to be very careful to spell words properly. One time, she had wanted to look up information and typed in D-O-L-L-F-I-N and instead of giving her information about *dolphins*, the browser had shown her a photograph of a doll with a shark costume on. She knew how to spell better now, however.

"*How to get rid of tangles."* She typed. She took some notes.

"*How to have less tangles.*" She wrinkled her nose and thought about it. She hit the backspace button and typed again.

"*How to have fewer tangles."* She smiled.

Computers were so *picky* about what kind of things you told them to do. Sometimes it was as bad as talking to a *baby*. If you didn't tell a baby what every single step was, exactly, they almost always got things wrong. Tansy had thought her tangles all morning during Sunday School. She thought about them for so long, and with so much concentration, that when Mrs. Johnston asked her what the name of Paul's friend in jail was, she dreamily replied, *"Hair."*

The class had laughed good-naturally. Mrs. Johnston regained her composure and replied.

"No, Tansy. We talked about Samson *last* week…" she continued to teach the lesson while blushing Tansy tried to pay attention to the rest of the class, but it had been *really* difficult.

Home finally, Tansy worked on her search. She looked up all sorts of interesting things and took so many notes on her three-punch paper that her hands started to hurt. She just *knew* if she had enough information, that she would be better at combing her hair and having less...no... *fewer* tangles to deal with.

CHAPTER SEVEN

Mrs. Joy looked at her nine-year-old daughter in amazement. The room was barely lit from the morning light outside. Birds were starting to sing. Tansy had woken her from a deep sleep and was standing next to her bed, peering down at her mom with a determined look.

"You want me to try what?" She repeated herself, trying to make sense out of the early morning conversation.

"I want to try these things that I found from the computer." Tansy asked again. "Please." she added.

Mrs. Joy rolled over to get her glasses. She peered at the clock. It read 6:03 *AM.* She looked over at her snoring husband. He would be heading to work in a few hours and Tansy had been studying up on hair de-tangling and styles all week long. Mrs. Tansy stretched, yawning. Mornings weren't her favourite, no matter what the reason.

"Tansy-Bear, if you'll let me get my cup of coffee, we'll work on this together."

Soon Tansy and her mom were working hard on her hair. They tried several different things to work on the tangles. The first thing they tried was to use a little conditioner in the ends to make the comb glide through more easily.

"I think that's a bust, Mom, it won't slide through properly" Tansy said. "Let's try the next thing. "They tried everything Tansy had found on her list. When the rest of the family was up, they all started making suggestions.

"Try just working the bottom part out first," suggested Dad, looking up from one of Tansy's note pages. They tried it. It seemed to help.

"I know!" piped up Zeb. "When I get my gym shoes wet, the laces get slippery. Maybe we should get Tansy's hair wet and then put that stuff in."

They tried that next. It seemed to help get the comb sliding in a bit better.

"This one says to use peanut butter!" Fauna shrieked, giggling. She looked at Flora.

"What does it say about jelly? I can get some!" Flora chimed in. This was fun.

"No peanut butter," Mom said firmly. "It's too

expensive already and I don't want it all over my couch."

"This one says to use a special brush." Flora read. "*By using the guilt-free tangle-beware brush, with extra combing action, you'll get rid of those pesky tangles in no time!*" She was unimpressed. "It says it takes three weeks to get here and it costs almost twenty dollars!"

Tansy nodded. "I saw that and I thought it was funny because it doesn't say *how* it takes the tangles out. If someone is going to sell you something, they should at least tell you how it works."

They were nearly done with Tansy's tangles.

"This one says to wrap it up in an old t-shirt." Said Zeb. "I have one in my closet you can use, Tans. Hang on."

He brought back an old *Ghoul-busters* T-shirt. It had a hole in the armpit.

"Hey!" said Dad. "That used to be mine! How did you get it?"

"Mom said it was old and it fits... I mean, it does look kinda raggedy Dad." Zeb replied.

"Well, at least it's getting some love and attention." Shrugged Dad.

Tansy had her hair de-tangled and was now wrapping it up, wet and filled with conditioner. It felt good to have her family helping with her tangles. She didn't feel quite so alone. She was glad that Mom was there too. She liked a good peanut-butter-and-dill-pickle sandwich, but the thought of peanut butter in her hair made her wince.

Tansy spent the whole day working on her hair and on her sisters' hair. She even worked on her Mom's hair. She tried several different styles, using their pretty clips and the bobby pin that she had won at the Farmer's Market.

By the time that Thursday was over, she was exhausted. Her arms were sore, her hands were sore, her eyes were sore. But you know, her hair? It wasn't sore. She had no hair headaches anymore and with all that practice, it seemed that she was finally past the fear of getting those tangles gone.

The doorbell rang. Granny Rice walked in. She had a special bag in her hand.

"Did I hear that *someone* has been working hard learning about different hairstyles?" she asked.

"Me! I have!" Tansy said, eyes wide. Granny seemed to know everything.

"Well I happened to look through my old linens - *that means towels and sheets and blankets dear-"* She said to nobody in particular. "And I found something that might help you tackle those tangles."

At this, Granny pulled out a pillowcase. It was different than Tansy's pillowcase. It was not soft and velvety. No, instead it was shiny and smooth. It had purple and pink flowers all over it.

"This is a satin pillowcase," Granny continued. "I found it tucked away in my things and thought you might get some use out of it."

Tansy hugged her Granny. "Thank you so much for this, Gran. That was something that my papers said was extra-helpful for keeping hair from getting extra tangles!"

Granny and Mom winked at one another.

"Better get to bed, kids." Mom said. "We've got a big day tomorrow."

Tansy went to bed, but all night she dreamed of horses and hairbrushes.

CHAPTER EIGHT

"Not only are tangled manes and tails a terrible mess, but they can also hurt your horse. Tangles and snarls can pinch and pull on the skin underneath. Tucked under the edge of your saddle pad at the *withers*, dirty, clumped tangles can even cause sores that may keep you from riding your animal while they heal." Mrs. Franzoso paused and took a sip of water, watching the serious faces of her students.

"It's important to make mane and tail care a regular part of taking care of your hose. You don't want to leave a tangled mess for so long that tangle troubles cut into your riding time." She continued. "Today, we're going to just work on the horses' mane. The student who does the best job combing out the horses' tangles and getting the horses hair into a style, will win the special prize!"

The kids all started chattering at once. They picked up the tools in front of them and then went to their favourite horses and began to work. Tansy walked up to Tiny. He was a mess. Somehow, she knew he had been rolling in the fields that morning, getting all kinds of junk into his long mane. She let him sniff her hand and then rubbed his softer-than-satin nose. He whickered at her and looked at Tansy, craning his neck and pawing the dirt, as if to say, 'Get on with it!"

Tansy took a breath. She looked at her notes.

"*One: Run your fingers through the mane and tail on a regular basis to work out any major snarls."* Tansy did this. There were a few places that had knots, but it definitely looked better than before.

"*Two: Hold your horse's mane in your hand while you brush, so that you're pulling on the root of the hair as little as possible. Use slow, smooth strokes instead of jerking your brush through the hair."* Tansy used slow, smooth strokes. She worked her way from the tip of the mane to the root, stepping up on a small stool in order to reach all the way to the top of Tiny's neck.

"*Three: Have fun. This is a good time to bond with your horse. Let him or her know you are their friend and you're there to help. Remember, they don't have hands to care for their hair by themselves."* Tansy smiled. She gave Tiny a hug. It was time to work on the fancy part. Tansy had practiced this fancy braid on her sisters for several hours the day before. The trick was to take your time and not rush. Very slowly, she took the horse's long mane and started what was called a *French braid.*

Tansy started by taking a small section of hair at the top of the mane by the *poll* and separated it into three strands. Then she began braiding. She was sure to braid over twice at the top to make sure the style held. Then, making sure she left a lot of hair at the bottom, she took a small strand of hair from the next part of the mane and added it to the strand closest to it. She added the strands over and over until she got all the way to the bottom. At the very end of the braid, Tansy put in her shiny silver bobby pin, with the dancing horse on the end.

Tired, but happy, Tansy stepped back and admired her work. Tiny's mane was tangle-free and the braid, which had evenly placed pieces, looked very tidy. The bobby pin set off the white mane perfectly. She finished up by wiping Tiny's coat with a rag to clear any extra dust off of his coat. She got every last speck of dust and grass off of Tiny and then waited, looking around at the other students.

Several of them seemed to be struggling to even get their horses' hair de-tangled. Duke, Jeremy's favorite, was putting his ears back nervously and pawing at the ground. Jeremy was getting red-faced and cranky.

"Come on, you silly horse!" Jeremy said, his hand open and pleading. "I just want to comb your burrs out!"

The rest of the students seemed to have similar issues. Only Jane seemed to really know what she was doing. Her horse, Bella, stood there, hair in several tiny buns, looking around for grass to munch on. Jane's nose was in another novel, so she wasn't really paying all that much attention. Tansy was glad she had taken the time to curry and wipe down Tiny. Bella's coat was still dusty in spots. Tansy then went to put all of her tack away. She made sure that Tiny was tied off to the fence, where he wouldn't be tempted to roll in the pasture. She had seen him eyeing it a few times during her hard work and didn't trust him to stay put.

"Well *that* was a good one." said Jane, putting her tack away next to Tansy's.

"A good what?" asked Tansy.

"A good *book*." Jane said. "It was all about elves

riding horses and fixing shoes."

"Oh." Tansy said. Books weren't her favourite thing. She'd much rather be *riding* Tiny than reading about him.

"Hey, that's a pretty hair thing." commented Jane. "Where did you get it?"

Tansy blushed. Here was *Jane*, complementing *Tansy* on her hairstyle. Before she could reply Mrs. Franzoso spoke up.

"Okay kids!" shouted Mrs. Franzoso. "I want you to finish up, then you can all go into the house for a special ice cream sundae treat, while I look at your work."

Everyone cheered. The kids finished what they could and then went inside, talking excitedly about the day's lessons. Tansy was so excited and nervous; she couldn't eat her ice cream properly. She felt like there was a whole herd of horses in her tummy.

CHAPTER NINE

I want to take time to talk about thoroughness." Said Mrs. Franzoso, as she watched the excited faces sitting in front of her.

"Thoroughness is something that is a very small thing, but also a very important thing to achieve. It means that when you do something, you do it all the way until it's done, and that you do it correctly- not taking any shortcuts." She looked down at a few students who were visibly squirming in their seats.

"*Some* of you today, did a good job getting tangles out, but you forgot some things- like making sure that your horse is wiped down properly after styling his mane. It's a lot like doing a beautiful hairstyle, but forgetting to wash your face." She smiled as several kids pictured this and giggled.

"*Some* of you did a beautiful braid, but you rushed ahead and forgot to get all the tangles out. That's not good for your horse. The tangles all have to be out before the mane can be styled." She paused.

"And *some* of you need to remember to tie your

horse up after you style their manes, because if they get to the pasture, they'll roll and undo all your work." At this she pointed to Bella, whose white coat was liberally smeared with green grass stains and her mane's buns were all bunched up with bits of grass and chickweed. She looked so comical, even Jane laughed.

"I guess Bella would rather she roll and I read!" Jane said.

"But one of you did such a great job with your horses' mane, I would like to show it off to everyone and give you the special prize. Tansy Joy? Would you come over here and get Tiny?"

Tansy practically bounced up. She walked over to Tiny, who was still carefully tied up to the fence, coat gleaming, and led him to where the students had gathered.

"Kids, look here and see what Tansy has done." Mrs. Franzoso pointed out. "Every last inch of his coat is shining, and she took a lot of time to slowly, carefully braid his mane. She even thought about how to decorate the style she made and included this fun little pin."

"A good horseman, or horse-girl, cares for their

horses, and takes time to make them shine. You wouldn't want to go to school or church and have your hair matted and messed up because you didn't follow through all the way getting it de-tangled and styled. You would want to put your best foot forward. Tansy has shown us all what hard work, good research, and a little practice can do. Great job, Tansy!"

Tansy blushed. She was excited, but she wasn't sure she liked to have everyone looking at her. Mrs. Franzoso handed her a little purple bag. It was about the size of Tansy's hand. She put it into her pocket.

"Thanks, Mrs. Franzoso!" Said Tansy. 'I couldn't have done it without Tiny!"

Tiny neighed and nodded his head as if to agree.

On the way home, Tansy peeked inside the little purple bag. Inside was another hair clip, exactly the right size for Tansy to wear and a western-style handkerchief to clip onto. There was a note attached.

Thanks for helping your horse look his or her best today! You did a great job and I'm proud of you! - Mrs. Franzoso

CHAPTER TEN

The next day was Saturday. The Joy family celebrated with a breakfast of waffles and quiche. Mr. Joy was overjoyed to hear the story of how Tansy had won the prize for best horse hairstyle. While Tansy basked in the cheers of her family, a knock came at the door.

It was a messenger with a package. The package was purple and it looked heavy. All eyes looked up at Mom and Dad as the kids tried to hide their curiosity. Mrs. Joy set the package on the coffee table and joined the family again for breakfast.

"Let's hurry up and finish, I want to tell you all some fun news." Said Mrs. Joy. She winked at Mr. Joy as he studiously finished his waffles.

Zeb bolted down the rest of his waffles, then looked over at Fauna's plate.

"Hey, I'm growing boy. Are you gonna eat that?"

Fauna looked at her brother and shook her head adamantly.

"Well I'm a growing girl and you can't!"

They all laughed.

As soon as breakfast was over, Mr. and Mrs. Joy called a family meeting. They all gathered together in the living room. Mrs. Joy opened up her purple box. Inside was at least *ten* hair accessories, designed a lot like the one that Tansy was wearing right now!

"Mom! That's so cool!" Said Tansy. Flora and Fauna immediately started looking through the hair accessories, trying to figure out what would look best in their hair.

Tansy saw something that caught her eye. It was a glossy paper that said, "*Opportunity Awaits.* It had a photo on the front of a lady dressed all in purple. She was grinning from ear to ear.

"What is all this?" Asked Tansy. "Was there a sale?"

Mom grinned. She looked over at Dad.

"Ahem." he started, his voice booming importantly. "We are all gathered here today.."

"*Jimmie…*" Mrs. Joy implored, eyes dancing.

"Oh, *right* dear." Mr. Joy grinned.

"Well kids, your mom and I talked and we've decided to add one more thing to our *Bucket List*. It's not going to be easy, we'll learn a lot, and I hope we'll have a lot of fun."

He took the pen and wrote on the *Bucket List* in big, loopy letters:

"Start a family business.'

"Any questions?" He asked, putting the lid back on the pen. It was going to be a great summer.

To receive a FREE copy of the first chapter of Book 2: "Flora Jean & The Money Mix Up" Be sure to sign up for The Joy Series Newsletter at www.nperrine.com.

Author's Note

Tansy Joy and Too Many Tangles began as a way to share with my own daughters my personal journey with my own very curly, very tangled hair. Growing up, I garnered little sympathy and was often made ashamed because of how my hair behaved. As though tangles and unruliness were something I could avoid, if I brushed often enough. It didn't help that my hair was becoming a source of preteen embarrassment at the time that the "Rachel" cut was making its world-debut. My envy of her chunky, straight locks knew no bounds.

When I became a mother of not one but *four* daughters (and one amazing son!) I started wondering what steps I could take to help my children have a positive view of their bodies, as early as possible. This would apply to everything, even their hair.

This started a journey that would lead to learning many things about a plethora of different textures and styles I even learned about other cultures' hair. In my research, I learned about many people groups and along the way discovered more about our unique genetic makeup. To my astonishment, I learned that Native American, French, English, Irish, Scandinavian, Spanish, Congolese and West African DNA had all blended together in our family over the years to make us who we are today. Rather than hide that rich family background, we've chosen to embrace those unique characteristics in our heritage.

In more recent years, I have learned much from a book written by Lorraine Massey given to me by a friend, and appropriately titled *"The Curly Girl Handbook."* It forever changed my view on my own hair.

Regarding the hair accessories that the "Purple Lady" sells at the Farmer's Market, you can visit my own website, www.lrose.biz/alabasterjar to locate those. I did, in fact, find the hair accessories that are described in the book, and they *absolutely* work on our kids as well as everyone I've met. They've become an *amazing* tool in our home, helping our daughters' "hair envy" go away, and helping each to embrace and celebrate what God has blessed them with.

Not only have the hair accessories been an added blessing in terms of usage, but the company, Lilla Rose, has been a complete joy and gift to our whole family.

I hope this book has blessed you and brought a little sunshine into your lives. Thanks for sticking it out to the end.

Niccole Perrine

About The Author

Niccole Perrine was born in Upstate New York, and raised primarily in Southern California and Southcentral Alaska. She now lives in Southwest Idaho with her husband, Luke. She is the oldest sibling out of of six and mother to five children, whom she educates at home. Her favorite hobbies include reading, writing, thrift shopping, and playing table top games with her friends and family.

About the Illustrator

Teagan Ferraby is a Painter, Illustrator, and Graphic Designer. She illustrates children's books and covers, specializes in sea life paintings and has been hired for commissioned artwork. She attends The Cleveland Institute of Art where she is working towards a BFA in Graphic Design. Teagan's inspiration comes mainly from her hobbies such as scuba diving, reading, and eco dyeing. Visit www.facebook.com/Teagansart and www.teagans-fine-art.jimdosite.com to explore her latest works of art.

Made in the USA
Monee, IL
22 March 2021